Lulu

and the Hedgehog in the Rain

Praise for *Lulu and the Duck in the Park*

2013 ALSC Notable Children's Book

☆☆☆

2013 Book Links Lasting Connection

☆☆☆

2013 Booklist Editors' Choice

☆☆☆

2013 Chicago Public Library Best of the Best

☆☆☆

2012 Kirkus Reviews Best Books of the Year

☆☆☆

2013 USBBY Outstanding International Book List

☆☆☆

2013 CCBC Choice

☆☆☆

2013 ReadKiddoRead Kiddos Finalist

☆☆☆

A Junior Library Guild selection

"McKay shows a rare ability to capture a younger audience in this involving chapter book for transitional readers. The well-structured, third-person narrative builds dramatic tension, provides comic relief of the most believable sort, and shows *plenty of heart*." —*Booklist* starred review

"A ***warmhearted*** beginning to a new chapter book series delights from the first few sentences…What Lulu and Mellie do to protect the egg, get through class, and not outrage Mrs. Holiday is told so simply and rhythmically and so true to the girls' perfectly-logical-for-third-graders' thinking, that *it will beguile young readers completely*." —*Kirkus Reviews* starred review

"McKay's pacing is ***spot-on***, and the story moves briskly. Lamont's black-and-white illustrations capture the sparkle in Lulu's eyes and the warmth and fuzziness of a newly hatched duckling. The ***satisfying*** ending will have children awaiting the next installment in what is likely to become a hit series for fans of other plucky characters like Horrible Harry, Stink, and Junie B. Jones." —*School Library Journal* starred review

"Many kids will sympathize with animal-loving Lulu, and McKay's easygoing, perceptive humor adds liveliness to the account…A lighthearted yet eventful outing, this will entice as a chaptery read-aloud as well as a read-alone." —*Bulletin of the Center for Children's Books*

Praise for *Lulu and the Dog from the Sea*

"Whether they live with dogs or not, readers will absorb some truths about family vacations and the true care of animal companions in the company of Lulu and Mellie, who are as **utterly charming** and as completely age seven as possible."—*Kirkus Reviews*

⋯⋯⋯⋯⋯⋯⋯⋯☆⋯⋯⋯⋯⋯⋯⋯⋯

"**Fresh as a sea breeze**, the story shows McKay's sure hand in creating characters, both human and canine. A rewarding addition to the Lulu series." —*Booklist*

⋯⋯⋯⋯⋯⋯⋯⋯☆⋯⋯⋯⋯⋯⋯⋯⋯

"**McKay hits the nail on the head** in this beginning chapter book...This title should be a staple in any early-chapter-book collection."—*School Library Journal* starred review

⋯⋯⋯⋯⋯⋯⋯⋯☆⋯⋯⋯⋯⋯⋯⋯⋯

"Like Lulu's first outing, this is rich in the guileless and eccentric charm that is McKay's hallmark, and the details of a family sorting out the difference between a dream vacation and a real one...will ring true to many readers." —*Bulletin of the Center for Children's Books*, recommended

Praise for *Lulu and the Cat in the Bag*

"This installment in the continuing story of Lulu, her cousin and best friend, Mellie, and her growing collection of pets delights...**It's very funny**." —*Kirkus Reviews*

⋯⋯⋯⋯⋯⋯⋯⋯⋯⋯⋯⋯☆⋯⋯⋯⋯⋯⋯⋯⋯⋯⋯⋯⋯

"McKay brings the characters to life in scenes full of warmth, wit, and perception...An ***appealing*** beginning chapter book from the ***excellent*** Lulu series." —*Booklist*

⋯⋯⋯⋯⋯⋯⋯⋯⋯⋯⋯⋯☆⋯⋯⋯⋯⋯⋯⋯⋯⋯⋯⋯⋯

"Another solid entry in this fine series" —*Horn Book*

Look for more books by

Hilary McKay

Lulu
and the Hedgehog in the Rain

Hilary McKay

Illustrated by Priscilla Lamont

Albert Whitman & Company
Chicago, Illinois

Library of Congress Cataloging-in-Publication Data

McKay, Hilary.
Lulu and the hedgehog in the rain / Hilary McKay ;
illustrated by Priscilla Lamont.
pages cm — (Lulu ; 5)
Summary: "When Lulu rescues a wild hedgehog in a storm,
she knows she can't keep it as a pet—it wants to roam free.
So she and her cousin Mellie come up with the neighborhood
Hedgehog Club to keep it safe"—Provided by publisher.
[1. Hedgehogs—Fiction. 2. Wildlife rescue—Fiction.
3. Cousins—Fiction.] I. Lamont, Priscilla, illustrator. II. Title.
PZ7.M4786574Lum 2014
[Fic]—dc23
2014013381

Text copyright © 2012 by Hilary McKay
Illustrations copyright © 2012 by Priscilla Lamont
First published in the UK by Scholastic Children's Books,
an imprint of Scholastic Ltd.
Hardcover edition published in 2014 by Albert Whitman & Company
Paperback edition published in 2015 by Albert Whitman & Company
ISBN 978-0-8075-4813-4

Printed in the United States of America.
10 9 8 7 6 5 4 3 2 1 LB 20 19 18 17 16 15 14

For more information about Albert Whitman & Company,
visit our web site at www.albertwhitman.com.

For Daniel Cooper.
I remembered how much your Great-Grandad liked
hedgehogs, and that gave me the idea for this story!
With love from Hilary McKay

Chapter One

The Wettest Day in Sixty-Four Years

Lulu and Mellie, who were cousins, were visiting their nan. It was an indoor visit because of the weather.

Lulu said, "This is the wettest day of my life!"

Nan thought about that. Lulu was seven years old. In those seven years, had there ever been a day as wet as this one? No.

"You're right!" she told Lulu. "It is the wettest day of your life!" Then Nan thought a bit longer and added, "I think it may even be the wettest day of my life too!"

"How old are you, Nan?" asked Lulu.

"Sixty-four," said Nan with pride. "Sixty-four, and I cannot remember a wetter day!"

"It's the driest day of my life," remarked Mellie, who was lying on the floor drawing, "because I'm not going out!"

"Wouldn't you like to, even for a minute?" asked Lulu.

"No, I wouldn't!" said Mellie, and she carried on drawing her picture of a desert with palm trees and camels and other dry things. She didn't like rain, and neither did Nan, but Lulu was fascinated. She couldn't stop looking out the window.

On that day, the wettest in sixty-four years, the rain fell from the sky in straight lines of water. In the garden the flowers were bent into puddles of brightness. The autumn leaves were washed down from the trees. The cars in the road left wakes of waves, like ships on the sea. The gutters beside the pavements bubbled like rivers.

Nan's three cats could not believe their eyes. They begged to go out and see for themselves.

"Don't be silly, cats!" said Mellie.

Lulu understood. She wanted to go out too. It seemed a waste to spend the wettest day in sixty-four years keeping dry indoors.

"I've got my rain boots and my umbrella," said Lulu, who had arrived at Nan's house wearing these things earlier in the day, when the rain had just been plain rainy rain, before it had turned into a flood.

"Don't be silly, Lulu!" said Nan.

So Lulu had to watch from the window for a little longer, until Nan and Mellie went into the kitchen to do some nice, dry baking.

Then, very quietly, Lulu picked up her umbrella, pulled on her rain boots, opened the front door, and stepped outside.

So did Nan's three cats.

One, two, three, they stepped outside.

Zip!

Zip!

Zip!

They turned and fled back in again.

That was enough rain for them.

It wasn't enough for Lulu. Carefully she closed the door behind the cats, and then she stood in Nan's little front garden and enjoyed the tremendous sound of a skyful of rain pounding down on her umbrella. In the road the cars flung up lace curtains of water as they passed. In the gutter, brown leaves twirled and surfed down to the drains. Lulu thought, *This is the most fantastic weather for sixty-four years!*

Then something else came tumbling down the gutter. Not surfboarding like a leaf, but rolling and bumping like a prickly gray ball.

"Oh!" gasped Lulu when she saw what it was, and she rushed out of the garden (which she was not allowed to do) and onto the pavement. Then she splashed across to the edge of the road, bent down, and scooped the poor gray ball out of the gutter.

It was a hedgehog.

"Ouch! Ouch! Ouch!" gasped Lulu, because a hedgehog, even a small and wet one, is not a comfortable thing to hold in bare hands. Still, she held on tight, and, leaving her umbrella behind on the pavement, ran back to Nan's house. The hedgehog took two hands to hold it safe. Lulu knocked on the door with her head.

"LULU!" cried Nan.

"Look what I've got! It's a hedgehog!"

"LULU, YOU TERRIBLE CHILD!"

"Could you just hold it a minute while I fetch my umbrella?"

"LULU, GET INSIDE THIS HOUSE THIS MOMENT! GOODNESS GRACIOUS, WHAT WILL YOU DO NEXT?"

All the time Nan was saying these things, she was putting on her boots, her coat, her hat, her gloves, and her

7

scarf. When they were on, she rushed upstairs and came back wearing the shower curtain like a shawl. Then she chose her largest umbrella, opened it, and stepped bravely outside. She was just in time to meet Lulu coming back with her own umbrella, rescued from the street.

"Lulu!" gasped Nan and zipped back in again, just like the cats had done a few minutes earlier.

"Is it still raining?" asked Mellie, appearing from the kitchen. Then she looked at Lulu and said, "Yes," and disappeared back into the warm again.

Water ran in streams from

Lulu's hair and face. It trickled from her sleeves. It puddled around her boots.

"Lulu," said Nan. "Go upstairs and take everything off! Drop it in the bath! Put on my big pink robe from the back of the bathroom door and come straight down!"

Lulu had vanished to do these things before Nan remembered something else.

"Lulu!" she called up the stairs. "Did you say *a hedgehog?*"

"Yes, but it's all right," called back Lulu as she dropped her sweater in the bath with a splash.

"What do you mean, all right?"

"Not dead!" shouted Lulu, squelching out of her socks.

"Have you taken it upstairs?"

"No," said Lulu, reappearing at the top of the stairs in Nan's robe. "I put it on the sofa."

"ON THE SOFA!"

"Just for a few minutes, while I went back for my umbrella. It won't fall. I put cushions all around. See!"

She was downstairs again now in Nan's tidy living room, gently lifting a green velvet cushion from Nan's silky gray sofa. There underneath was a large patch of damp and in the middle of the damp was a small curled hedgehog.

"Hmm!" said Nan. "Next time, Lulu, you think it is a good idea to leave a half drowned hedgehog on my sofa, please wrap it in a towel first."

"Sorry, Nan," said Lulu, but she could tell that Nan was not really mad. She was looking at the hedgehog very kindly.

The hedgehog was trembling so hard its whole spiky little ball of a body rocked on the sofa. Every now and then, tight in its ball, it sneezed.

"Aww!" said Mellie.

They wrapped it in warm towels and took it into the kitchen and Lulu tried to remember everything she knew about hedgehogs.

"There was a show on TV all about them," she said. "They live wild around here, like squirrels and mice, but not everywhere. They like to eat cat food, and they come out at night. Maybe they don't like brightness."

In case it didn't like brightness they found it a shoebox and put it inside, away from the light. That seemed to be a good idea. At last the trembling slowed down, and the hedgehog began to uncurl. It stuck its nose in the air and snuffled and sneezed while Lulu and Mellie and Nan watched and whispered.

"What is it sniffing?"

"Us, I suppose."

"Us!" said Mellie indignantly. "We don't smell!"

"To a hedgehog we do."

Mellie sniffed her hands. They smelled slightly of sharpened pencils. She sniffed Nan, who smelled of coconut, and Lulu, who smelled of rain. Then, very cautiously, she sniffed the hedgehog.

"Worse than wet dogs!" said Mellie.

"I like the smell!" said Lulu, who liked everything about animals, even things that other people did not like at all.

"What are you going to do with it?"

"Take it home," said Lulu, and she sounded so surprised to be asked the question that Nan and Mellie laughed. Then Nan went away to take off her shower curtain and Mellie went back to her drawing and Lulu was left alone with her hedgehog. She leaned over the box and sniffed.

"Lovely!" she said.

At the end of the day Lulu went home with the shoebox with the hedgehog inside. She also had some cat food borrowed from Nan's cats for the hedgehog's supper; some flea powder, also borrowed from Nan's cats, for just in case; her still-damp sweater; and her rain boots in a shopping bag.

Lulu dropped everything except the shoebox just inside the door and carefully put the box on the table.

"You'll never guess!" she told her parents.

"There are air holes in the box lid,"

said Lulu's mother, "so we might!"

"It's something we've never had before!" said Lulu very proudly.

Lulu was always appearing with animals in need of help. Stray dogs, unwanted rabbits, spare guinea pigs, noisy hamsters and goldfish-grown-out-of-their-bowls had all found happy homes at Lulu's house. A tortoise lived in the garden and a parrot lived in the

kitchen. It was hard to think of anything that they had never had before.

Lulu's father said he supposed it must be a smallish armadillo.

"That's almost right!" said Lulu, and then she took off the box lid and showed them the hedgehog she had found in the rain. They gazed and said, "Oh, how wonderful!" and "Just as good as an armadillo!" and Lulu smiled happily.

But the hedgehog did not seem happy. It sneezed and trembled and ate nearly nothing. A lick of cat food from the end of a teaspoon, that was all.

Perhaps it got seasick, sailing down the gutter like that! thought Lulu. Seasick and bumped and frightened and cold. No wonder it wasn't hungry.

When Lulu went to bed that night,

the hedgehog went too, tucked up in the box beside Lulu's pillow. And every time Lulu heard a rustle or a sneeze she thought, *Good! Still alive!*

All the next morning the hedgehog slept, and the sleep made it better. The sneezing stopped, and in the afternoon it woke up and ate a large late lunch. Soon it was well enough to climb out of the shoebox and go exploring in Lulu's bedroom. That was what was happening when Mellie came up the stairs.

"It looks loads better!" said Mellie.

"It is!" said Lulu proudly. "It got so much better after it had something to eat that even its fleas got better! Jumping!"

"Oh," said Mellie, backing down the stairs very quickly.

"Don't worry, we flea-powdered them,"

said Lulu. "Poor fleas. But I don't think the hedgehog minded. What it needs now is somewhere to live. I thought we could make it a little house in the garden."

"And we have to think of a name too," said Mellie.

"We can do both together," said Lulu, scooping the hedgehog back into its shoebox again. "Let's start right now! Come on!"

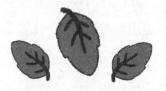

Chapter Two

Sonic-for-Short

The house that Lulu and Mellie built
for the hedgehog was at the very end
of Lulu's garden, against the garden shed.
The shed made one wall. Old
bricks made the others.

A spare roof tile was
propped so it would
keep out the rain.

Inside they put dry leaves
and hay from the bag that Lulu kept for
her rabbits and guinea pigs.

 19

"It's a bit scruffy though," said Mellie worriedly. "Won't the hedgehog escape without a door? And what about things to play with like you give to the rabbits?"

Lulu looked at Mellie in surprise. She had not realized that Mellie thought the hedgehog was going to be a pet, with toys to play with to save it from boredom and an escape-proof door.

"This hedgehog is a wild animal," she explained. "All hedgehogs are wild where we live. It won't need toys or a door because it'll be able to go in and out whenever it likes. It'll have the whole garden."

"It doesn't seem safe," said Mellie, but when she looked around the garden she saw that it was safe. Lulu's garden had a fence all around. If the gate was closed, there was no way out.

"And it won't get lost," admitted Mellie, "because the garden's so little. We still need a name. What have you thought of?"

"I wondered if we should call it after Nan."

"You can't call a hedgehog Nan!" protested Mellie.

"Not Nan! Cherry! That's Nan's real name."

"Cherry's not a very hedgehoggy name!"

"What is, then?"

Mellie lifted up the shoebox lid and looked at the hedgehog.

"Pineapple," she said.

"Pineapple!"

"Or Prickles."

"Almost every hedgehog in the world is called Prickles," objected Lulu.

There was a pause while Lulu and Mellie patted hay and leaves into a comfortable bed and tried to think of a name that no hedgehog in the world had yet been called.

"Bubbles!" said Lulu.

"John!" said Mellie.

"John? John! Are you crazy?"

"John Cherry Bubbles Pineapple Prickles," said Mellie. "Five names, like the queen of England!"

"The queen is called Elizabeth," said

Lulu. "Come on, Hedgehog! Come out and see if you like your new house!"

She tipped the shoebox gently and the hedgehog came hurrying out at once, its black-currant nose twitching. In and out of the little house it went, and then off around the garden.

"Queenie," said Mellie. "John Cherry Bubbles Pineapple Prickles Elizabeth Queenie!"

Then Mellie got the giggles and had to lie on the ground.

"Crazy!" said Lulu, scattering her with autumn leaves. "Hey, Mellie, we're surrounded! Look!"

Faces had suddenly appeared: two on one side of the garden, one on the other, Lulu's neighbors peering over their fences to see what all the fuss was about. Arthur on one side, Charlie and his friend Henry, who lived a little farther down the street, on the other. Lulu and Mellie knew them well. They were all in the same class at school together.

"What have you got?" asked Arthur. "Another rabbit?"

"A hedgehog!" said Lulu proudly.

"A hedgehog?" repeated Henry, and Charlie asked, "A live hedgehog? I've only ever seen squashed ones! Where?"

Lulu pointed to where the hedgehog was busy snuffling under a rabbit hutch, and all three boys at once scrambled over their fences and into the garden.

"I've always wanted to meet an actual hedgehog!" said Henry excitedly. "I don't believe they're as prickly as they look!"

"They are," said Mellie, who had said the same thing only the day before, but all three boys insisted on crawling under the rabbit hutch and testing for themselves.

"Hey, Sonic!" called Arthur, while Henry reached out a fascinated, frightened finger.

"Careful!" warned Charlie.

Henry could not have been more careful if he had been about to poke a crocodile.

"It stings!" he said, wriggling backward
as fast as he could.

"Come out now before you scare it!"
said Lulu. "And it's not called Sonic either!"

"What's it called, then?" asked Arthur.

"We're still choosing," said Lulu quickly.

"Sonic's a great name," said Arthur.

"Sonic the Hedgehog. I've got the game for my XBox!"

"Is it going to live here, then?" asked Charlie.

"Yes. Wild in the garden."

"Oh, it's not fair!" burst out Henry. "I've only got one fat boring hamster! I want a hedgehog! Where do you get them?"

"You can't just get them," said Lulu.

"You did!"

"I found it," explained Lulu. "Washed away in all that rain."

"What about a swap, then? You can have my hamster!"

"No!" protested Lulu.

"My hamster and my Tyrannosaurus rex!" said Henry. "It only needs new batteries!"

"No!"

"What, then?" demanded Henry, who was used to getting his own way.

"Nothing," said Lulu. "Anyway, it's not mine to swap. It's a wild animal! It belongs to itself. It's just living here, that's all!"

"What if it wants to live somewhere else?"

"It likes it here," said Lulu.

At first this seemed true. The hedgehog seemed happy and it soon grew used to people. Every evening, at the clink of the food plate, it came out of its house to eat up its supper, before trundling off in search of slugs and snails and wood lice and other hedgehog treats. By the time Lulu went to bed it would have vanished into the shadows. But it always came back. Some time during the night, while the humans were asleep, the hedgehog would return to the little house and put itself to bed. In the mornings, if

Lulu bent very close to the little house, she could hear the magical sound of a hedgehog snoring.

"Sleep tight, Hedgehog!" she whispered.

She and Mellie still hadn't agreed on a name.

Then things began to change. The hedgehog no longer seemed quite as happy in Lulu's garden. It seemed to want to visit Charlie's as well. It found a tiny

gap under the fence in between, and it would not leave it alone.

It scraped and scratched until it had quite a large hole. Almost a way through. Lulu filled the hole with stones, which made her feel even worse than flea-powdering the fleas had done. The stones did not stop the hedgehog. Bit by bit, pushing and digging, it began working on the hole again.

Lulu and Mellie worried. They spent a whole afternoon in Lulu's bedroom, worrying and worrying.

"John Cherry Bubbles Pineapple Prickles Elizabeth Queenie Sonic-for-Short is being so silly!" said Mellie.

"It's what hedgehogs do," said Lulu.

"Be silly?"

"No! Wander! Look at this book. It tells you."

It was a book
that Lulu had
found in the library
at school. It was
a book entirely
about hedgehogs.
Lulu had read
the whole thing,
and now she
knew more about
hedgehogs than she
ever had before.

"One garden isn't
enough," she told
Mellie. "Especially
a little garden
like ours. It says a proper wild hedgehog
needs much more space than that. But
if we let the hedgehog go through to
Charlie's garden, then what?"

"Then it'll be lost," said Mellie.

There was a map in the hedgehog book. It showed the track of a hedgehog exploring at night.

Mellie began drawing a map of her own. She drew Lulu's garden and Arthur's garden and Charlie's garden. She drew the fences in between. Mellie drew her lines hard and black because she was upset. She said, "I thought we were going to look after the hedgehog."

"We are," said Lulu.

"Well then, we should fill in that hole and not let it make anymore. It could have a lovely run to play in like the rabbits have. We could put in leaves and branches and things to explore. Then it would be safe."

"Then it would be a pet hedgehog, not a wild hedgehog," said Lulu. She pulled

Mellie's map toward her and asked, "What comes after Charlie?"

"The New Old Lady."

"Oh yes."

Mellie took her map back and continued her drawing. She murmured as she drew.

"Arthur's garden, Lulu's garden, Charlie's garden, New Old Lady's garden…" (They called her the New Old Lady because she had just moved into the street.) "Empty garden, Bossy Man's garden, Henry's garden…"

Mellie drew wiggly lines to show where the gardens were divided by hedges, and straight ones to show where there were fences. After Charlie's garden there were only hedges.

"See how far the hedgehog could go if it gets under the fence," said Mellie. "All the way to Henry's!"

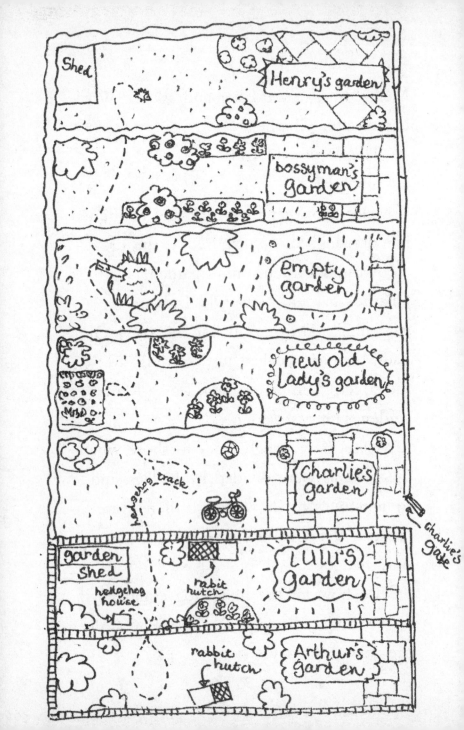

"That's what a wild hedgehog should be able to do," said Lulu.

"It wouldn't be safe. Even going as far as Charlie's wouldn't be safe. Their gate is open all the time. It would get out onto the road."

"Not if Charlie shut it."

"How do you know the New Old Lady would care about hedgehogs?"

"How do you know she wouldn't? We could ask. We could go and talk to her."

"What, and go and talk to the Bossy Man too? I don't want to!"

Lulu didn't want to either. The Bossy Man was almost always grumpy. He tried not to be, but he was. He liked peace and quiet and tidiness. It was unlucky for the Bossy Man that he lived where he did, next door to Henry. It made him bossier and grumpier than ever.

"Henry is the worst of all," said Mellie. "He wants the hedgehog for himself."

"Nobody can have that," said Lulu.

"No, because it's yours."

"Not really. I'm just trying to look after it. But I can't on my own, in one little garden. What if everyone helped, you and me, and Arthur and Charlie and Henry, and the New Old Lady and the Bossy Man as well…If we had a hedgehog club…"

Mellie, who had been drawing hedgehog footprints all around the edge of her map, rolled over and looked at Lulu.

"A hedgehog club?" she asked.

"Yes, for people who would keep their gardens hedgehog-safe."

"A proper club, like the *Doctor Whatsit* show fan club at school? They have badges. The Hedgehog Club could have badges! I could make them with my badge-making machine!"

"Do you think it's a good idea, then?"

"If I can make the badges I do."

"You can make the badges. We'll give them to everyone who says they'll help."

"Free badges for hedgehog clubbers!" said Mellie. "And I know what! Free maps of the gardens to show them how important they are! I love drawing maps! Who'll we ask first?"

"Charlie," said Lulu at once, "because before the hedgehog can go anywhere we've got to make Charlie start shutting his gate."

Chapter Three

The Hedgehog Club

Charlie's garden had a gate that drove his family crazy. It was an ordinary gate. It opened and closed like any other gate. But it was open much more than it was closed because Charlie could never remember to shut it.

Trash blew in and annoyed his mother. Stray dogs wandered in and bothered the cat. Once a football burglar burgled Charlie's big brother's brand-new football.

"Shut the gate, Charlie!"

"Charlie! The gate!"

"Come back, please, Charlie, and…"

But as often as not, before they stopped speaking, Charlie would have vanished.

Late for school.

Rushing down to Henry's.

Wobbling on his skateboard.

And there would be the gate, left open again.

Getting Charlie to join the Hedgehog Club was not easy. Lulu and Mellie went around to his house after school and at first he was very stubborn.

"I don't like clubs," he said. "They kicked me out of that *Doctor Whatsit* one and I'm never joining any more again!"

"We won't kick you out; we want you in!" said Lulu. "The Hedgehog Club is a great club! No kicking out and free maps and badges!"

Charlie still was not happy. He looked at his free map and insisted on drawing himself on it. He looked at Mellie's badges and said, "No way! 'I heart hedgehogs'! I'm not wearing that!"

"If I make you a different badge, will you join?" asked Mellie.

"What else do I have to do?"

"Shut your gate!"

Charlie said he wasn't going to be told what to do.

"We're not," said Mellie. "We're just saying you've *got* to remember to shut your gate!"

"That's telling me what to do!" said Charlie sulkily. "Anyway, I almost always do."

"You almost always don't!" said Lulu.

"So Mellie's made you a special notice to put on it to remind you."

Mellie was good at art. Her notices were bright and bold. Charlie's said in fierce red letters:

SHUT THIS GATE!

"How bossy!" said Charlie.

"Charlie," said Lulu. "It's really important!"

When Lulu said important, Charlie's face changed. It looked interested for the first time.

Lulu and Mellie made a new notice.

Very Important!
Please keep Charlie's Gate Shut!

And Mellie made a new badge, especially for Charlie. SHARP! NOT FLAT! said the

badge she made,
around a picture
of a very sharply
prickled hedgehog
indeed.

"That's better!"
said Charlie, and he
was in.

Henry was the next person they asked. At
first he could not understand it.

"But you're letting it go!"

"Sort of."

"When you wouldn't even swap?"

"Only if we can make a hedgehog club
to keep the gardens safe."

"My garden's safe. It's got walls all
around except for the Bossy Man's side
and the gate shuts itself."

"Good."

Henry looked at his map. With his finger he traced a line from Lulu's garden to his.

"It could come straight to me."

"It could go anywhere," agreed Lulu.

"OK," said Henry. "I'll join! Where's my badge?"

Mellie had made him a wonderful badge. KEEP SPIKY! it said, with a picture of a hedgehog with its spikes arranged in a way that looked very like Henry's own hair.

"Cool!" said Henry.

Arthur was easy. Mellie did him all by herself when Lulu wasn't listening.

"Do you want to join our hedgehog

club to help look
after Sonic-for-
Short?" she asked.

"Yes," said Arthur.

Arthur's badge said
TEAM SONIC!

"Good name!" said Arthur.

"Sonic?" asked Lulu doubtfully when she
heard.

"Sonic-for-Short!" said Mellie.

"Oh all right!" said Lulu. "Who next?"

"I think the New Old Lady," said
Mellie. "I think you should leave the
Bossy Man till last!"

Lulu noticed that she said "you" and
not "we."

"The New Old Lady might be even
worse than the Bossy Man," she said.

"Let's ask Charlie what she's like,"

suggested Mellie. "He should know. He lives next door."

Charlie was helpful. He had not lived next door to the New Old Lady for long, but he knew all about her.

"She's nice," he told Lulu. "She's very nice to our family anyway! She has to be!"

"Why?"

Charlie explained that the first thing the New Old Lady had done after coming to live next door was to reverse her car into his dad's motorbike.

"It was parked outside our house where he always puts it," said Charlie. "And she said she didn't see it! She bashed it down and then she ran over it! And then she came around all in a flap and we had to give her a cup of tea."

"But why does that make her have to be nice?" asked Lulu.

Charlie explained. His family had been nice about the motorbike. Now the New Old Lady had to be nice back. She had to throw back footballs. She had to put up with Charlie and Henry's rock band practices.

"And she'll have to join the Hedgehog Club!" said Charlie. "I'll come with you to ask her if you like, to make sure."

Charlie was right. There never was a nicer old lady. She came smiling to her door to talk to Lulu and Mellie and Charlie. She loved her I HEART HEDGEHOGS badge and she said she always kept her gate locked so they needn't worry about that.

"We used to have a

hedgehog in the garden when I was a girl," she told them. "Dear little things!"

"Yes, they are," agreed Lulu. "And useful. Sonic-for-Short will eat up your slugs and snails for you too."

"Don't talk to me about slugs and snails!" groaned the

New Old Lady. "This garden is full of the beasties! I've been putting down slug pellets. I must have killed hundreds already!"

"Oh please don't do that!" exclaimed Lulu. "What if Sonic-for-Short ate slug pellets by mistake? Or some of the poor poisoned slugs?"

"Oh, that would never happen," said the New Old Lady cheerfully. "Bread and milk! That's what hedgehogs like best! Your little hedgehog won't bother with slugs and snails if it has bread and milk for supper. It will be nice to have a hedgehog to feed again... Oh! Goodness! Where has she gone?"

Charlie and Mellie couldn't guess. Lulu had dashed away without a word of explanation. She returned a minute later, and flopped down panting on the doorstep.

"I went for my hedgehog book," she said, hurriedly turning pages. "Look!

It tells you everything! Where they live…making houses…how to tell their footprints from cats and rabbits and things! Here's a bit about hibernation (that's when they go to sleep all winter) and here's what they eat. Slugs. Snails. Wood lice. Beetles. No bread and milk! It makes them sick! It tells you! See?"

"We always put out bread and milk," protested the New Old Lady.

"If you want to feed them you should give them cat food," said Lulu. "That's what this book says. That's what we do."

"You'd have all the local cats around," said the New Old Lady. "I don't want that! I'm not feeding cats."

"Don't you like cats?" asked Mellie.

"We've got a cat," said Charlie.

"Oh yes. I forgot." The New Old Lady sounded tired of being nice. She said in a not-very-joking voice to Lulu, "Are you going to sit there on the doorstep and read the whole book?"

"Please would you not put out bread and milk for Sonic-for-Short, please?" begged Lulu. "And not poison the slugs and snails in your garden anymore?"

"How else can I get rid of them?" asked the New Old Lady.

"I could come with a bucket," offered Lulu. "We all could! The Hedgehog Club! We could collect your slugs and snails and take them home. That's a good idea, isn't it?"

The New Old Lady gave up. She agreed to no bread and milk and she agreed to snail collecting and then she shut her door very quickly, as if she didn't want to have to agree to anything else.

"I told you she was nice!" said Charlie,

and Lulu said, "Yes," but Mellie looked thoughtful.

"Slugs and snails in a bucket?" she asked after a while.

"What could be easier?" asked Lulu cheerfully.

Mellie did not reply.

After the New Old Lady there was only the Bossy Man left.

"I can't go with you," said Mellie to Lulu. "He doesn't like me or Arthur. He moaned to our moms about the chalk pictures we drew in the street."

Charlie wouldn't go either. He had once accidentally thrown a football shoe through the Bossy Man's windshield. He wished he hadn't. The Bossy Man wished he hadn't. But neither of them could ever forget it.

"I'm not
going," said
Henry. "He's been
complaining ever
since I got
my trampoline!"

"Why?"

"He says I keep
appearing. Pulling
faces. It's just my
trampolining face!"

"It's 'cause you cross your eyes," said
Mellie.

"Not on purpose."

"And stick out your tongue!"

"Everyone does, jumping."

"And waggle your fingers with your
thumbs in your ears!"

"Anyway, I'm not going near him,"
said Henry, and Arthur and Charlie and

Mellie said the same,
but Mellie also added
something very sensible:
"Ask Nan!"

Nan was the
answer. She liked
the Bossy Man. She
liked his garden. She
understood completely about
chalk all over the pavement and shoes
through windshields and trampolining
neighbors with terrible faces. She and the
Bossy Man talked about these things as
he tidied his garden. They talked about
how to prune roses too, and the way the
leaves blew in from the park down the
road, and how hard it had rained on the
day of the hedgehog rescue. And before
he knew it, the Bossy Man had joined
the Hedgehog Club too.

"You don't need to worry about my gate," the Bossy Man told them. "I keep it locked because of the ki…"
He paused, looked at Lulu, and tried again. "…wind! Is that for me?"

Lulu nodded and handed him his badge.
SONIC-FOR-SHORT RULES!
Mellie had written around a picture of a hedgehog in a crown. (The crown had been Lulu's idea. "Just right for such a bossy man," Mellie had agreed.)

The Bossy Man put his badge in his pocket with the map wrapped around it and said he would look at them both later, when he had finished raking the leaves.

"Thank you," said Lulu, and she went home with Nan very happily. Later, she went down to Sonic-for-Short's hedgehog house to whisper the news.

"We've made you a hedgehog club, so you can be a wild hedgehog! You can go as far as you want to now. All the gardens are safe."

"Brrrr!" went Sonic-for-Short's tiny snore.

There was one star out in a purple sky. There was the cheerful sound of voices coming from the park. There was a lovely smell of damp grass and bonfire smoke in the air.

Bonfire smoke! thought Lulu, and she remembered the Bossy Man's pile of raked-up leaves. Then she leapt to her feet and ran.

"What? What?" demanded the Bossy Man as she hurtled down his garden path.

"You can't have bonfires!" shouted Lulu.

"WHAT?"

"You might cook a hedgehog!"

"WHAT?" said the Bossy Man.

"They hide in piles of leaves just like that!"

"Remind me of your name!" said the Bossy Man.

"Lulu."

"Lulu, there is no hedgehog in this pile of leaves. I know. I raked them up myself, only this afternoon. You were here. You saw me."

"I didn't see you rake up the whole pile."

"Well, I did."

"All of it this afternoon?"

"Almost."

"Was there a little pile to start with?"

"Yes, but there was no hedgehog in the little pile."

"Did you check?"

"Not under every leaf," admitted the Bossy Man, and he began to put out his bonfire, raking and stamping until he was left with nothing but great piles of smoky damp leaves all over his garden.

"What am I to do with them?" he grumbled.

"Couldn't you just leave them on the grass?"

"Of course not!"

"Or put them in the trash?"

"Not allowed!"

"They blew here. Perhaps they will blow away again."

"I don't think so."

"You know the New Old Lady?" asked Lulu.

"No."

"The one who squashed up Charlie's dad's motorbike."

"Go on!"

"The Hedgehog Club is taking away her slugs and snails so she doesn't use poisonous slug pellets. Would you like us to take away your leaves as well?"

"Where to?"

"My garden. In the wheelbarrow. It would be easy!"

"Are the slugs and snails going there too?"

Lulu nodded.

"What do your parents say about that?"

"They don't mind," said Lulu cheerfully. "I take home all sorts of things. They never mind. Even when I took home four rabbits all at once they didn't. I'm always looking for new things for my rabbits to play with. They'd love your leaves!"

The Bossy Man stood thinking for a very long time.

"All right," he said at last. "You take

my leaves for your rabbits. I'll give up
the bonfires. We'll see how it goes."

"The Bossy Man is giving me all his
leaves for my rabbits," Lulu told her
father as she brushed the dogs that night.

"All of them?" asked her father. "All of
them! All those great heaps that blow in
from the park?"

"Yes. It's so he doesn't have to burn
them in a bonfire. It's a Hedgehog Club
thing."

Lulu's father groaned and her mother
asked, "Are there anymore Hedgehog Club
things we should know about?"

"There's closing the gates," said Lulu,
ticking them off on her fingers. "But
we always do because of the dogs. Not
having bonfires. No giving them bread
and milk because it makes them sick. And

the New Old Lady's slugs and snails. Poor
little things."

"Why are they poor little things?"
asked Lulu's mother.

"Because she's been feeding them
poisonous slug pellets," said Lulu. "She's
killed hundreds! She told me! But she's
not killing any more. They're coming
here to live instead. The Hedgehog Club
is going to collect them every day."

"Oh are they?" said Lulu's mother.
"Well, please don't show them to me
when you bring them home. It all

seems like a lot of work for one small hedgehog. Are you sure Mellie and the boys will help?"

"They'll love to," said Lulu.

Chapter Four

Autumn

After school was a busy time at Lulu's house. There was home-work to do, the two dogs to play with, and the rabbits and guinea pigs to feed. There was a

tortoise whose old brown shell needed polishing with olive oil and a parrot to be sprayed with a mist sprayer to remind him of long-ago African rains. And now there were slugs and snails to collect and gates to check and leaves to wheel in barrow loads from the Bossy Man's house.

There was a tunnel now under the fence to Charlie's garden, and another on the other side, dug by Arthur and his father. That was nice of Arthur's father, who had just put a new fence all around his garden.

"He likes hedgehogs," said Arthur. "And he said to tell you not to forget the pond in the empty garden. He says it should have a ramp so that if Sonic-for-Short falls in he can get out again, and he said to let him know if you want a hand making one."

The pond was something Lulu had forgotten, and she was very glad Arthur's father had remembered it. She helped Arthur and his father make a ramp out of a spare piece of wood and an old rubber doormat cut into strips, and all three of them crept into the empty-house garden to put it into place.

"How do hedgehogs survive in the wild?" asked Lulu's father. "With no one to feed them cat food and collect them slugs and snails and rescue them from bonfires and make them houses and ramps and tunnels? Not to mention the leaves! How many more thousand tons of leaves do you think will fit into this garden?"

"Are you really mad?" Lulu asked him.

"Am I ever really mad?"

"No," said Lulu.

At night, when Sonic-for-Short came out, every moment of trouble was worth it. Lulu smiled with happiness as he rustled through the dry leaves and explored under the ivy. Slowly, slowly the hedgehog, a little round shape in the evening shadows, made his way to the gap under the fence.

Then, suddenly, he was gone.

"He'll be quite safe," said Lulu to comfort herself. "He's being a wild hedgehog. He's doing what hedgehogs do."

All the same, in the night Lulu often
woke up to stare out her bedroom
window, wondering. And in the
mornings she could not wait to race out
into the garden.

Had Sonic-for-Short come home?
Would there be snoring or not?
Snoring!
There was definitely snoring.

"He came home safe! He came home
safe!" called Lulu to her parents at
breakfast, to Nan down the phone, to
Mellie and the boys on the way to school.
"We let him go and he came home safe!"

Day after day Sonic-for-Short came
home safe.

"It's working!" said Lulu. She was so
pleased that she didn't care how many

leaves she wheeled away from the Bossy
Man's garden. She didn't mind how
many slugs and snails she collected from
the New Old Lady. She didn't mind
how grumpy Charlie became when she
reminded him to close his gate. She
didn't even mind that Henry was being
suddenly mysterious.

"I can't help with the leaves," he told
Lulu and Mellie, "or the slugs and snails. I'm
busy. So's Charlie. Hedgehog stuff. Soz!"

"Soz!" said Mellie, staring. "Soz! Did
you say soz?"

"Yeah, soz! You know, sorry," said
Henry. "I'll show you when it's finished!"

Henry swaggered away with his hands
in his pockets. With his spiky hair and his
puffy jacket and his little short legs he
looked so like a hedgehog himself that
Lulu could not stop laughing.

"Soz!" said Mellie again. "Henry is just not cool enough to say soz instead of sorry! And what is he going to show us?"

They found out the next day. A hedgehog house. A hedgehog house in Henry's garden.

"A luxury hedgehog house!" said Henry proudly.

All of Henry's family had helped to make it. Henry's father was a carpenter; there were lots of spare pieces of wood stacked behind Henry's shed. Henry's mother had given him her old window shade for a roof. It had a pattern of bunches of grapes all over. Henry's grandma found him a fluffy purple bath mat to use for a carpet, and a matching purple towel for a hedgehog bed. Even Henry's hamster was useful. Hamster treats were heaped in a corner.

"They were my idea," said Charlie.

"It's a palace!" said Lulu.

"Fantastic!" said Arthur.

"Very purple," said Mellie.

"I like purple," said Henry. "But the best thing about this hedgehog house is, anytime I want to know if anyone's inside I can just take off the roof!"

Henry took off the roof to show them.

"I wouldn't like that," said Lulu, "if I

was at home asleep in bed and a giant came and took the roof off to see if I was in!"

"I'd love it," said Henry, and he took off the roof several times a day.

Sometimes Charlie's cat Suzy was inside.

"See!" said Henry. "Animals like it!"

Suzy had been very pleased to discover a private purple den with hamster treats inside, but she hated having the roof taken off. She rocketed away at the sound of Henry's footsteps.

"If Sonic-for-Short comes to live here, you won't keep taking the roof on and off, will you?" asked Lulu anxiously.

"Only very carefully," said Henry.

Without meaning to, the Hedgehog Club had divided into different jobs for different people. Arthur checked the pond ramp. Charlie closed his gate. Henry added luxury extras (like doormats and a chimney) to his purple palace. Lulu and Mellie collected leaves and slugs and snails.

"We do the most," said Mellie. "Unless you count Arthur's XBox," she added enviously. The boys counted playing *Sonic the Hedgehog* on Arthur's XBox as Hedgehog Club work. They did it every day after school.

"Lucky things," said Mellie.

The leaves did not take long, but the slugs and snails took ages, especially the way Mellie collected them. Mellie did not like touching slugs and snails. She picked them up with a spoon.

"Forty-six, forty-seven, forty-eight…" counted Lulu, as she dropped snails into her snail-collecting bucket.

"Two, ugh! Three…" counted Mellie.
"Lulu, Lulu, help! They're climbing up
the sides of the bucket again!"

The New Old Lady covered her eyes
at the sight of Lulu's bucket and said,
"You are very brave girls!"

"You won't forget about no bread and
milk?" Lulu reminded her.

"No, but it does seem ridiculous!" said
the New Old Lady. "Our hedgehogs
always ate bread and milk."

"Should I get my library book again?"

"No, no, no!" said the New Old Lady hastily, and hurried indoors.

Every evening now, Sonic-for-Short set off on his trip around the gardens. He explored them all. In Arthur's he posed for photographs. At Charlie's he met Suzy, who jumped backward, bristling in horror. In the New Old Lady's he was dazzled by flashlight, as the New Old Lady inspected her visitor.

"He's very small," she said to Lulu the next day. "Ours was twice the size!"

"What happened to yours?" asked Lulu.

"Oh, vanished, like they do," said the New Old Lady. Lulu patted her hand and did not say what she thought.

"I've seen her several times," said the
Bossy Man, when Lulu visited to collect
his leaves. "Are you sure
you want all this trash for
those rabbits?"

"Oh yes!" said Lulu.

"I've been pruning
as well. There's a
great pile of sticks."

"Rabbits like sticks to bite on," said Lulu. "It's good for their teeth. I can take them too if you like."

Henry hadn't seen Sonic-for-Short in his garden, but that was not surprising. He never seemed to see anything until he walked right into it. He had stopped putting hamster treats in his hedgehog house because Suzy ate them.

"Suzy eats anything except cat food," said Charlie proudly. "Ice cream, jam, chips, and cheese!"

Henry heaved the roof of his hedgehog house and peered inside.

"Still no hedgehog," he complained.

"He does come to your garden, though," said Lulu.

"How do you know?"

"Hedgehog poo," said Lulu. "Look! All under your trampoline!"

76

"What! That's disgusting!"

"I thought you'd be pleased!"

"Why did you show me? Now every time I jump I'll be thinking about poo!"

"I thought you wanted Sonic-for-Short in your garden!"

"I do! I just don't want poo!"

Henry gave another disgusted look at his trampoline and said, "Anyone who likes can borrow it!" stomping off to his shed. He came out again carrying his skateboard.

"I'm fed up of this Hedgehog Club," Lulu overheard him complaining to Charlie later that afternoon. "Poo everywhere!"

"I'm fed up of being nagged about our gate," Charlie replied. "The second Lulu hears it squeak she comes around roaring like a tiger!"

"I thought you'd started climbing over it."

"I have, but it's no good with a bike..."

"The boys have stopped wearing their Hedgehog Club badges," Lulu said to Mellie a few mornings later.

Mellie, who wasn't wearing hers, looked guilty.

"And the Bossy Man never did. He just put it in his pocket."

"Nan wears the one we made for her," said Mellie.

"That's because she's Nan, not because of the Hedgehog Club," said Lulu. "She wears it like she wore those pasta earrings we made her. And the acorn necklace, and the scarf you wove her out of parts of socks."

"Nan loved that scarf!" said Mellie. "I made it specially on that weaving thing she gave me. I don't know why everyone laughed at it."

"They didn't."

"You did."

"Only because I recognized the socks."

Mellie sniffed.

"What's the matter?"

"I've got a cold," said Mellie. "And…"

There was a pause while Mellie waited for Lulu to ask "And what?"

Lulu didn't.

The pause became longer.

"Slugs and snails!" said Mellie suddenly.

"What about them?"

"Picking them up with spoons!"

"Mellie?"

"Every day after school I think 'Oh good! I can go home!' and then I think, 'Oh no! I can't. I've got to go and pick up slugs and snails with spoons!'"

"I thought you liked it!"

"OF COURSE I DON'T LIKE IT!"
shouted Mellie.

"Oh."

"And now I've got this cold and I don't
think it would be good for me."

"It would! Fresh air!"

"I don't want fresh air," growled Mellie. "I want to go home and watch TV!"

Lulu became a Hedgehog Club on her own.

It was true that Nan wore her badge whenever she came to visit.

The New Old Lady smiled and asked for Hedgehog Club news.

The Bossy Man resisted the great temptation to light bonfires.

Charlie continued to climb over his gate.

Mellie asked, almost every day, "How's Sonic-for-Short?"

Henry still looked carefully under his trampoline before he bounced on it.

Arthur began to save up for *Sonic the Hedgehog 2*.

But that was as hedgehoggy as they got.

Leaf collecting, slug-and-snail hunting, and washing up the empty cat-food saucers were left to Lulu alone. The nights got darker and slugs and snails became harder to find. The pile of the Bossy Man's leaves and sticks in Lulu's garden grew enormous. Lulu's father looked at them unhappily. Lulu's rabbits did not look at them at all. The New Old Lady hinted more than once that warm bread and milk would be just the thing for a small cold hedgehog these chilly evenings.

And then Sonic-for-Short vanished.

Chapter Five

Winter

When?

Lulu did not know. There were two
days of wind when no one could have
heard an elephant snore, never mind
a small hedgehog. And then the wind
was mixed with icy rain, so cold it was
nearly snow. And in the middle of all this
weather Lulu became ill. Her throat hurt
and her eyes were sore and she ached
all over, and then she began to sneeze
and sneeze. So she was put to bed with

ice cream and tissues and terrible yellow medicine from the doctor. And Mellie was kept out of the way in case she caught it too.

While Lulu was ill she could not look after her pets. The tortoise was asleep for the winter in a box of hay, but the rabbits and the parrot, the guinea pigs, and the two bouncy dogs all had to manage without her. Her parents looked after them instead.

"And Sonic-for-Short too?" croaked Lulu when she was well enough to speak.

Her mother and father looked at each other, and then rushed outside with a double helping of cat food and left it by Sonic-for-Short's house.

"Was there snoring?" croaked Lulu.

"What?"

"If you bend right down next to his house you can hear him snoring."

"Lulu, do you know it is almost snowing out there?"

"Is it?"

"Sleeting and howling!"

"Can I go and see?"

"NO!" said Lulu's mother and father, but Nan, who had come over to see how the invalid was, actually

picked her way down to the end of
the garden and bent down to the
hedgehog house and listened.

She was a good nan.

"I think I may have heard something,"
she told Lulu. "It was hard to tell, but I
think I might!"

*In the morning I can see if the cat food has
been eaten,* thought Lulu as she lay in bed
that night.

In the morning the cat food looked like
terrible half-frozen soup. Hungry birds
had found it and left dozens of footprints
in the icy mud. It was impossible to tell
whether a hedgehog had been there too.

"When can Mellie come and see me?"
asked Lulu in despair.

"Poor Mellie's got this as well, now!
Try and eat your soup!"

Lulu ate her soup. She swallowed her medicine. She tried so hard not to cough she nearly exploded.

"I'm better!" she announced, long before she really felt like doing anything but lying on the sofa, and before anyone could stop her, she wobbled outside.

She couldn't hear snoring.

The latest saucer of cat food had not been touched.

How long had it been since she had last seen Sonic-for-Short?

More than a week!

Had Charlie's gate been left open any time in that week?

"Are you still going on about that?" asked Charlie grumpily.

"Yes."

"I didn't leave it open. I suppose it might have blown open."

"Did it blow open?"

"It might have. A little."

Lulu checked the pond in the empty garden. The ramp had half sunk and was covered in slippery fallen leaves.

"You forgot about Sonic-for-Short!" said Lulu to Arthur.

"Forgot!" said Arthur. "Forgot! Do you know I spent almost all my birthday money on *Sonic the Hedgehog 2*!"

"I didn't forget her!" said the New Old Lady proudly. "But I thought you'd lost interest in the poor little thing!"

Lulu shook her head.

"Anyway, I remembered!" said the New Old Lady. She sounded pleased about something. She sounded like someone who was about to explain they had been right all along.

She did.

"Every night this week I've put out a nice large plate of bread and milk!" she told Lulu. "And every morning it has all disappeared! So what do you think of that?"

The Bossy Man was just as bad.

"Bonfires?" he asked. "You think I've been making bonfires in this weather? I shoveled up the last of the garden stuff and put it in the trash."

"I thought you said the garbage men wouldn't take it," said Lulu.

"I bought them some doughnuts," said the Bossy Man. "Then they did."

"Oh," said Lulu, and then she said, "I think the hedgehog is lost."

"Ah," said the Bossy Man. "A pity."

"You couldn't have shoveled him up with your garbage?"

"No," said the Bossy Man.

"Are you sure?"

"Absolutely. Almost absolutely."

"Almost?"

"Yes, almost."

No hedgehog ate the saucers of cat food
anymore. No small round shape hurried
out into the dusk. One evening, the
New Old Lady discovered Suzy the cat
gobbling bread and milk.

"Was it you all the time?" cried the
New Old Lady.

Suzy licked her
milky jaws
and smiled.

"Shoo!" cried the New Old Lady angrily. "I'm not feeding cats!"

So that was that.

Still Lulu did not give up. One morning, when the air was so still and frosty you could hear the leaves as they fell one by one from the trees, she spent a long time listening beside the hedgehog house.

Mellie found her there.

"It's almost tumbled down," Mellie said, looking at the little house. "If you didn't know what it was, you wouldn't know what it was! Can you hear anything?"

"I'm not sure," said Lulu. "Perhaps hedgehogs don't always snore. Perhaps sometimes they just do very quiet breathing."

"Couldn't you reach inside and see if you could feel him?"

"No! Because what if I woke him up?

You shouldn't wake up hibernating animals. Sometimes they can't go to sleep again. Then they die."

"Anyway, I don't think he's there," said Mellie, after bending down to listen for herself. "I can't hear a thing. And where else could he be?"

Lulu didn't answer, but she thought of the Bossy Man's trash-bagged leaves. She thought of the pond with the ramp out of place and she thought of Charlie's gate.

But also she remembered Henry's purple palace.

93

Perhaps, perhaps, perhaps, thought Lulu, Sonic-for-Short was safely tucked up in Henry's purple palace.

Chapter Six

Spring

One day Lulu's two bouncy dogs bounced on the nearly tumbled-down hedgehog house and it collapsed completely. There was no hedgehog inside.

Mellie hugged Lulu and did not say "I told you so."

Lulu thought, *It might still be all right. There is still Henry's.*

She did not dare say this thought out loud. She didn't want Henry taking off the roof of the palace to check. She just hoped.

Lulu hoped all winter. All through the exciting days coming up to Christmas. All through the dark of January. All through the snow that followed. All through the long wet thaw.

Everyone else forgot the hedgehog, but Lulu kept waiting and hoping until spring.

One day in early spring Lulu's father took a long look at his garden and he said, "It's the worst in the street!"

It was. Several horrible-looking cat-food saucers. The Bossy Man's sticks, all blown around. The Bossy Man's leaves, a great dark slimy heap. The hedgehog house all tumbled down.

"Time to tidy up!" said Lulu's father.

The saucers were washed.

The sticks were gathered.

A roll of garden trash bags appeared, and a shovel and a rake.

"The Bossy Man said if you give the garbage men doughnuts they will take it away," said Lulu.

"I don't think I could afford all the doughnuts they would want to take this," said Lulu's father. "I'll drive it down to the recycling center."

He shoveled for ages while Lulu and Mellie held open the bags and raked the scattered leaves back into heaps. While they were busy Arthur and Charlie and Henry arrived.

Then at last Lulu said what she had been hoping all winter.

"Do you think Sonic-for-Short could be at your garden, Henry?"

"Who?" asked Henry, staring. "Oh, I remember! No."

"Not in that house you made?"

"Definitely not!"

"Are you sure?"

"'Course I'm sure," said Henry. "Me and Charlie took that house apart ages ago to make jumps for our skateboard park."

Then everybody saw Lulu's face.

Lulu's father took charge. He got the boys out of the way by making them help him carry the filled-up bags up to his car. He gave Mellie the shovel and Lulu a hug and said, "You two rake up those last few leaves! I'll take it all away and come back by the pizza place. We'll have a pizza party because... because...Help me out here, Mellie! Why do we need a party just now?"

An early bee flew across the garden.

"Because it's spring," said Mellie, and she began to hurry with her raking to get the job done.

But Lulu watched the bee. She watched the bee and sniffed a lot and rubbed her eyes and felt a warmth in the sunshine that she hadn't felt for months, and then she heard Mellie say, "Lulu!"

"I'm all right," said Lulu. "I'm not crying if that's what you thi—"

"No! No! Lulu, look! First I thought it was an old brush or something...Lulu, *please* look!"

So Lulu gave one last sniff and one last

rub and turned to look and it was Sonic-
for-Short.

Under the last of the leaves, deep
in a hollow, as if he had
melted into the ground.

Sonic-for-Short.

And they could see
him breathing.

Lulu and Mellie fell to their knees.
They stared. They thought of the winter

that the hedgehog had survived. Winds so strong they blew Charlie off his bike. Christmas all alone. Freezing cold and frost and snow.

They fetched the boys and the New Old Lady and the Bossy Man. They telephoned Nan.

"Wonderful!" said Nan.

"Excellent!" said the Bossy Man.

"Amazing!" said the New Old Lady. "They usually disappear!"

Lulu thought of the times to come. More snail collecting, more worrying, more battles. Then she looked up and she thought, *Perhaps not so many battles.*

The Hedgehog Club was back in action. Charlie had run to close his gate. Arthur had dashed away to check the ramp in the pond.

Henry was staggering back from the
car with a sack of leaves. The Bossy Man
helped him to tip them out. Mellie and the
New Old Lady began sorting out the driest.

Gently Lulu began to tuck up the
sleeping hedgehog with handfuls of leaves.

The boys fetched a second bag, and then a third. They piled them around her. Then they told each other *Shush!* and tiptoed away.

And after that the Hedgehog Club had a pizza party, because it was spring!

Turn the page for a
sneak peek at the next

Lulu

adventure!

When Lulu goes for a sleepover at her nan's
house, she isn't supposed to take her new
hamster. But how can she leave him behind?

Chapter One

Ratty the Hamster

Lulu was seven years old, and she was famous for animals. She was so famous for animals that people buying new pets for their children had begun to say,

Well, if things go wrong we can always ask Lulu to take it.

Lulu did not know they said this, and neither did her mom and dad. They might have minded, or they might not. Lulu's parents were quite famous themselves, for letting Lulu have so many pets. They said, *The more the merrier! As long as Lulu cleans up after them.* Lulu did not just clean up after them. She looked after them as if they were the most important things in the world.

And to her, they were.

At Lulu's school there was a big girl called Emma Pond. Emma Pond had a hamster. Emma Pond's hamster had a hamster wheel. The hamster ran desperately on the hamster wheel, hour after hour, day after day, week after week. It ran as if it was trying to escape. Whenever it got off the wheel it would look around as if to say "Am I still in the same place?" When it saw that it was, it tried again.

The hamster wheel made a squeaky noise that Emma Pond did not like. She used to reach through the bars with a pencil and poke the hamster off the wheel.

One day, when Emma Pond's hamster had the chance, it bit Emma Pond. This happened on a day when Emma had not been able to find a pencil and had used her finger to poke him instead. It was not a little bite; it was a big one. As big as the hamster could manage.

The next day Emma Pond came up to Lulu at school and said, "I'm getting rid of my hamster."

"Why?" asked Lulu.

"How?" asked Mellie, who was seven years old like Lulu and her best friend as well as her cousin.

Emma Pond answered them each in turn. She unpeeled a sticky bandage from her finger and showed Lulu two red holes. "That's why," she said. She told Mellie, "I'll just let it go if Lulu doesn't want it."

"Let it go where?" asked Lulu.

"Perhaps at my uncle's. He's got a big field. We let our rabbits go there."

"What happened to your rabbits?"

Emma Pond shrugged to show she didn't care. "Anyway," she said to Lulu, "my house is on the way to yours. You could stop on your way home."

"Today?" asked Lulu.

"Today, after school," said Emma Pond. "Wait at my gate. If you're not there, I'll know you don't want it."

"I want it! I want it!" said Lulu.

Right after school that day Lulu and Mellie rushed to Emma Pond's house.

"Wait!" commanded Emma when they reached the gate. Then she went in and came back carrying a small plastic cage.

Inside the cage was a heap of newspaper and hamster bedding and a hamster wheel. The rubbish heap twitched a little.

"Is it a boy or a girl?" asked Lulu.

"We never really…" began Emma Pond,
and then she stopped. "It's a boy," she
said. "Or if it's not, it's a girl. Obviously."

"What's its name?" asked Mellie.

Emma Pond paused. It was almost as if
she didn't want to tell them. Then she said,
"Ratty!"

"Ratty?" repeated Mellie.

"Ratty?" echoed Lulu. "But you said it was a hamster!"

"That's right."

"Called Ratty?"

"Are you taking him or not?" demanded Emma Pond.

"We're taking him," said Lulu.

Lulu and Mellie walked home, carrying the cage between them. With her free hand Mellie held her nose.

"I don't think Emma Pond has cleaned this cage for weeks and weeks and weeks," she said.

At Lulu's house they put the cage down on the doorstep and stretched their arms.

"We still haven't seen a hamster," said Mellie, but even as she spoke, the heap of newspaper in the cage began to move. A pink nose came out. A ginger head with bulging eyes. It yawned, showing curving orange teeth. Next Lulu and Mellie saw a ginger body with a bare patch of skin in the middle and last of all, a short hairless tail.

Then Lulu and Mellie and the ginger-colored animal all had a good stare at one another. While they were doing this, Lulu's mother came out.

"What's *that*?" she asked.

"It's a hamster," Lulu replied, and she explained about Emma Pond and Emma Pond's bitten finger and the field and the rabbits and the way Emma Pond had shrugged when Lulu had asked what happened to them.

"Well," said Lulu's mother at the end of all this, "I don't see what else you could do but bring the poor little animal home! What's its name?"

"Ratty!" said Mellie.

"Oh," said Lulu's mother. "Oh!" And then she had another look in the cage and said, "Oh. I wonder what Nan will say."

Collect all the *Lulu* adventures!

**Lulu and the
Duck in the Park**
HC 978-0-8075-4808-0
PB 978-0-8075-4809-7

**Lulu and the
Dog from the Sea**
HC 978-0-8075-4820-2
PB 978-0-8075-4821-9

**Lulu and the
Cat in the Bag**
HC 978-0-8075-4804-2
PB 978-0-8075-4805-9

**Lulu and the
Rabbit Next Door**
HC 978-0-8075-4816-5
PB 978-0-8075-4817-2

**Lulu and the
Hedgehog in
the Rain**
HC 978-0-8075-4812-7
PB 978-0-8075-4813-4

**Lulu and the
Hamster in
the Night**
HC 978-0-8075-4842-0

About the Author

Hilary McKay is the eldest of four girls and grew up in a household of readers. After studying zoology and botany in college, Hilary went on to work as a biochemist. She became a full-time mother and writer after the birth of her two children. Hilary says one of the best things about being a writer is receiving letters from children. Hilary now lives in a small village in England with her family. When not writing, she loves walking, reading, and having friends over to visit.